Billy's Sister:

Life when your sibling has a disability

By Jessica Leving

For all the siblings out there...

Hi! My name is Jessica, and this is my little brother Billy.

Billy and I are just like most brothers and sisters. We play together, watch movies together, and laugh together.

And of course, sometimes we don't get along. But a little arguing and being angry with each other is normal for kids in all families— it's called sibling rivalry.

6

For the most part, me and Billy are a lot like any brother and sister. But one thing that makes us special is that Billy has a disability. It's sometimes called having special needs.

There are lots of different kinds of disabilities—and just like people without them, people with disabilities are all different. Some might use wheelchairs, others might use hearing aids, or others might even have cool computers that talk for them.

Billy's disability is a little harder to see, because he doesn't use any special machines or tools. It's called autism.

Having autism makes lots of things challenging for Billy that are easy for me. He learns a lot more slowly than other kids his age at school, and sometimes has trouble with things like following directions, staying quiet in public places like movie theaters or the library, and making friends.

It isn't his fault—but that doesn't mean it isn't still frustrating once in a while.

Like for instance, when I have friends come over, sometimes I worry about what my friends might think. It can be hard to try and explain Billy's disability, or answer questions about why he behaves the way he does.

Or other times, when I want to play with Billy, he just sits there and ignores me. Sometimes he even goes and plays with our parents, instead of me! I know Billy's autism can make it hard for him to play the same way that other kids do… but I'm not just any other kid! I'm his sister! Shouldn't I be the one who's most fun to be around?

15

I feel really guilty about it, but sometimes I even get mad at Billy just for not understanding things. It can be SO annoying when I tell him something over and over in as many different words as I can think of and he just doesn't get it. It makes me want to scream!

17

So, sometimes… I do.

And then, I usually get in trouble.

A lot of times, it feels unfair that Billy gets special treatment because of his disability. It can feel like he gets all the attention, and no one ever blames him for doing anything wrong—even when it really is completely his fault and *I* would totally get in trouble if I did the same thing. Grrr.

My mom says having a sibling with a disability means I have to grow up a little faster than other kids. She tells me I should be grateful that I understand things more quickly than he does and make friends pretty easily.

And usually, I am! But sometimes… I'm just not so sure. He gets away with EVERYTHING!!!

Having a sibling with a disability can be really, really hard. And it's okay to be upset about it sometimes. Not just okay, in fact—it's completely normal! I've never heard of *any* siblings who have a 100 percent perfect relationship.

Disability or not, each and every family is different—and, even if it might not seem like it, *every* family has their struggles.

As Billy's sister, I know Billy in a way that no one else does. All siblings have special relationships different than the ones they have with their parents and friends, and Billy and I are no different. We still hang out together, play tricks on our parents, and know the best ways to bug each other AND make each other smile.

Billy's autism can be challenging to deal with, but it's also taught me a LOT—about patience, about love, and about respecting the differences in people.

I've also discovered how helpful it can feel to write my feelings down, or draw a picture when I'm feeling mad or sad. You could even say being Billy's sister is part of how I decided to become a writer!

No matter how frustrating things can feel sometimes, I will always love my brother. And you know what? I wouldn't give up being Billy's sister for the world—disability or not.

THE END

Jessica Leving wrote *Billy's Sister* based on her real-life experiences growing up as... you know, Billy's Sister. The first draft of this book was written when she was in high school, at the request of a local social service agency that was looking for resources to share with siblings of kids with disabilities.

Now both grown-ups, Jessica and Billy continue to be as close as ever.(And they still love pranking their mom!)

In addition to the book, Jessica also hosts a podcast on sibling issues and speaks to community groups about how they can support sibs.

Wiem Sfar is a Tunisian artist who lives in Singapore. After studying interior and graphic design, 3D modeling and 3D animation, she specialized as a freelance illustrator and graphic designer. She enjoys combining her art with humanitarian service, so she really enjoyed working on the *Billy's Sister* cover and illustrations (especially after designing the *Evely's Sister* book cover and illustrations, too!).

If you wish to see more of her work or to contact her, please visit: ***www.wiemsfar.wixsite.com/design***

This book was created as a project of The Center for Siblings of People with Disabilities. For more resources—including My Sibling Story, *our companion workbook created to help kids process feelings and spark meaningful family conversations —visit **www.siblingcenter.org***

Made in United States
Troutdale, OR
08/28/2023

12436919R00021